Gifts for Gus

The Sound of G

By Peg Ballard

The Child's World®, Inc.

Gus got a lot of gifts.

Gus got a toy car.

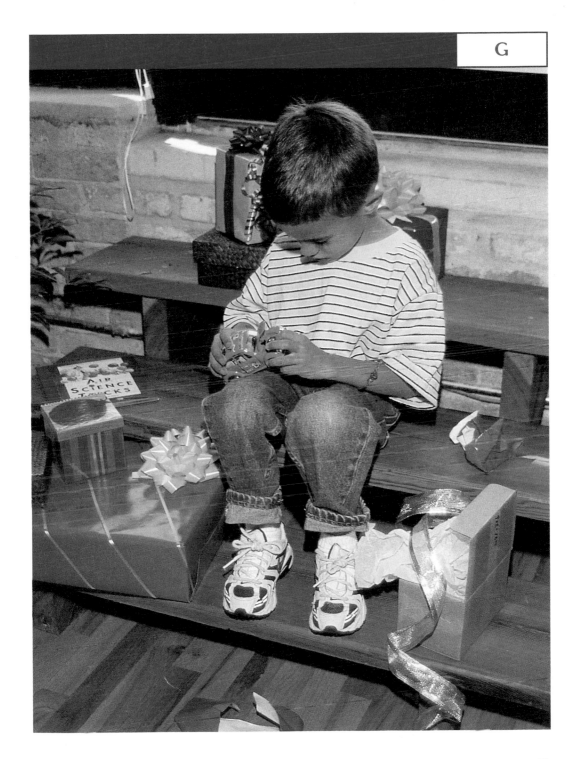

Gus got a pet goldfish.

Gus got a red wagon.

Gus got a book.

Gus got a new ball.

Gus got new boots.

Gus got gumballs.

Gus got a gold hat.

Gus got many good gifts.

Word List

gifts	got
gold	gumballs
goldfish	Gus
good	

Note to Parents and Educators

The books in the Phonics series of the Wonder Books are based on current research which supports the idea that our brains are pattern detectors rather than rules appliers. This means children learn to read easier when they are taught the familiar spelling patterns found in English. As children encounter more complex words, they have greater success in figuring out these words by using the spelling patterns.

Throughout the 35 books, the texts provide the reader with the opportunity to practice and apply knowledge of the sounds in natural language. The 10 books on the long and short vowels introduce the sounds using familiar onsets and rimes, or spelling patterns, for reinforcement. For example, the word "cat" might be used to present the short "a" sound, with the letter "c" being the onset and "-at" being the rime. This approach provides practice and reinforcement of the short "a" sound, as there are many familiar words made with the "-at" rime.

The 21 consonants and the 4 blends ("ch," "sh," "th," and "wh") use many of these same rimes. The letter(s) before the vowel in a word are considered the onset. Changing the onset allows the consonant books in the series to maintain the practice and reinforcement of the rimes. The repeated use of a word or phrase reinforces the target sound.

The numbers on the spine of each the book facilitate arranging the books in the order that children acquire each sound. The books can also be arranged into groups of long vowels, short vowels, consonants, and blends. All the books in each grouping have their numbers printed in the same color on the spine. The books can be grouped and regrouped easily and quickly, depending on the teacher's needs.

The stories and accompanying photographs in this series are based on time-honored concepts in children's literature: Well-written, engaging texts and colorful, high-quality photographs combine to produce books that children want to read again and again.

Dr. Peg Ballard
Mankato State University

Photo Credits

All photos © copyright Romie Flanagan/Flanagan Publishing Services

Special thanks to the Fahrenbach and Koutris families

An Editorial Directions Book
Photo Research: Alice Flanagan
Design and production: Herman Adler Design Group

Library of Congress Cataloging-in-Publication Data

Ballard, Peg.
    Gifts for Gus : the sound of "g" / by Peg Ballard.
      p. cm. — (Wonder books)
    Summary : Simple text and repetition of the letter "g" help readers
learn how to use this sound.
    ISBN 1-56766-701-5 (lib. bdg. : alk. paper)
    [1. Gifts Fiction. 2. Alphabet.] I. Title. II. Series: Wonder books
(Chanhassen, Minn.)
PZ7.B21195Gi   1999
[E]—dc21
                                          99-20962
                                            CIP